Maisie's Magical Ch. ...

by
Jon Markes

illustrations by
Nicky Jones

First published 2022

Santa's Trousers Books,
Cleggs
6 Goodramgate, York, YO1 7LQ

cleggsyork.com
info@cleggsyork.com

This is a story about a Reclaimer called Maisie. Each Reclaimer is very individual, handmade by Nicky from Cleggs from paper and clay and dressed in clothes made from reused fabrics.

The Reclaimers are a group of characters who care for the environment. They are creative people who make things from other people's rubbish and bits and pieces collected from nature.

Maisie loves making and has been invited to have a stall at this year's Christmas market. She is very excited and also a little nervous.
She is working hard to get everything ready in time.

Maisie's Magical Christmas

Maisie is in her workshop making decorations to sell on her Christmas market stall. She is surrounded by pieces of fabric, wool, cardboard, twigs, leaves and other bits and pieces she has been collecting all year.

All day long, Maisie has been stitching, knitting and gluing. She is about to finish for the day when she hears a *squeak* coming from the basket of fabric scraps in the corner.

Maisie looks into the basket and sees a small mouse sitting on top of the scraps.

'Oh, hello,' says the mouse.

'What are you doing in there?' Maisie asks.

'I'm collecting fabric,' says the mouse.

'Why are you collecting fabric?' asks Maisie.

'To make clothes,' replies the mouse.

'You use my scraps of fabric to make clothes?'

'Yes,' says the mouse. Then, in a slightly embarrased voice, 'I hope you don't mind.'

Maisie laughs. 'Of course I don't mind! You're doing what we Reclaimers do - taking things that have been thrown away and making them into something beautiful.'

The mouse scrambles up the side of the basket and stands on the rim. Maisie shakes the mouse's hand.

'I'm Maisie. What's your name?' she asks.

'My name's Mervyn Mouse,' he says.

'How did you get into my workshop, Mervyn Mouse?' asks Maisie.

Mervyn Mouse points to a mouse-sized hole in the wall, behind the coat rack.

'Through the hole in the wall over there,' he says.

'Well, you don't have to climb into the basket of scraps. I can save them for you,' says Maisie.

'Really?' says Mervyn Mouse.

'Really!' laughs Maisie.

'I'm busy making decorations to sell on my Christmas stall, so there will be lots of fabric for you. Come to see me on Wednesday afternoon and I'll let you have plenty.'

Mervyn Mouse squeaks excitedly.

'Thank you, Maisie. You're very kind!'

With a wave, he scuttles away to the woodland village where he lives.

The next Wednesday, Mervyn Mouse, Cinnamon Rabbit, Margie Mouse and Hector Hare arrive at Maisie's workshop.

Small bundles of fabric are stacked neatly in the corner.

'We can make lots of clothes with all this fabric!' says Hector Hare.

'There's enough to make blankets,' says Cinnamon Rabbit.

'And cushions,' says Margie Mouse.

'And pants!' adds Mervyn Mouse.

'Pants!' repeats Hector. The villagers burst out laughing and Mervyn blushes.

'Thank you, Maisie,' say the villagers as they leave.

'You're very welcome,' says Maisie. 'Come again next week. I have so many things to make. There will be plenty more scraps for you.'

The villagers arrive back in the village with their bundles.

The next Wednesday, the villagers appear at Maisie's workshop.

However, there is no stack of fabric in the corner, only a few scraps.

Maisie is at her workbench crying. Her arm is in a sling and she is surrounded by half-finished Christmas decorations. Some have not been started at all.

The villagers gather around the workbench.

'What's happened, Maisie?' asks Mervyn Mouse.

Maisie sobs. 'I tripped over in the workshop and hurt my arm. I only have two days to finish making everything before the Christmas market begins. I haven't been able to make anything all week and all the other Reclaimers are busy getting their own stalls ready!'

'It'll be alright, Maisie,' says Cinammon Rabbit, 'you've already made lots of lovely things.'

'It's not enough!' cries Maisie.

The animals look at each other wondering what to do.

'We need to go to Agnes Mouse and tell her what's happened,' whispers Mervyn Mouse.

The villagers knock on Agnes Mouse's door. They tell her all about Maisie and her poorly arm.

Agnes Mouse listens very carefully and thinks for a while.

After a minute or two, she says, 'we must help Maisie. Find out which of the villagers can make things. Ask them to meet me here in one hour!'

One hour later a crowd of enthusiastic villagers has gathered outside Agnes Mouse's house.

'This is wonderful!' exclaims Agnes Mouse, clapping her hands. 'Let's go to Maisie's workshop!'

The villagers arrive at Maisie's workshop. Maisie is looking worried and feeling very sorry for herself.

She is surprised when the villagers march through her door.

Agnes Mouse jumps onto Maisie's workbench.

'Don't worry, Maisie. We're here to help you!'

'Help me? How?' asks Maisie.

'If you tell us how to make the decorations, we can make them for you.'

'But there's so much to do. You can't make everything in time for the Christmas market.'

'Yes, we can,' says Mervyn Mouse, 'we work very fast!'

Maisie looks around the workshop at the half-finished decorations. She asks the villagers what they are good at doing.

'I can knit,' says Shona Sheep.

'I can sew,' says Margie Mouse.

'I'm good at making wreaths,' says Finley Fox. 'We have a wreath making competition every year in the village.'

'I can make pants,' says Mervyn Mouse. 'Colourful pants!'

The Giggling Mice are playing with some white, fluffy pompoms Maisie was making before she hurt her arm.

'Can we make pompoms?' they giggle.

'Well, if you like pompoms, I can show how to make them,' says Maisie, cheering up a little.

'What do you think, Maisie?' asks Agnes Mouse. 'Can we help you?'

Maisie looks at the villagers with eager looks on their faces.
'I think that would be wonderful!'

For the next two days, Maisie's workshop is buzzing with activity.

Maisie tells each of the villagers what to do and they set to work. They are very excited about learning new skills.

There's lots of singing, cutting, sewing and sticking.

Maisie's mother fetches tea and mince pies from the house.

'Has anyone seen the Giggling Mice?' asks Hector Hare.

The villagers shake their heads.

Then Maisie hears giggling coming from under her workbench.

She lifts the cloth and a pile of white fluffy pompoms spills out. Right in the middle of the pompoms sit the Giggling Mice.

'Do you think we've made too many!' they giggle and everyone laughs.

Just before midnight on the second day, all the Christmas decorations are finished ready for Maisie to sell on her stall.

The villagers pack them into boxes to take to the Christmas market in the morning.

Maisie stands at her workbench, a big smile on her face.

'Thank you all, so much,' she says.

'We'll be back in the morning to help you take everything to your market stall,' says Agnes Mouse.

The villagers, tired but happy, leave Maisie's workshop. As they walk back towards the village, they pass the row of market stalls.

The stalls are all brightly decorated, except for one which is drab looking and empty - Maisie's stall.

'Oh, no!' cries Agnes Mouse. 'Look! She points to the stall, looking sad among its brightly decorated neighbours.

'We can't have that,' says Mervyn Mouse, 'we must do something!'

They talk to the Nelly the Knitter and her dog, Hank, who offer to find some lights and decorations for Maisie's stall. Walter the Woodworker lets the villagers use his ladder to reach right to the top.

The villagers set to work stringing up rows of lights and garlands.

Before the sun rises, Maisie's stall is the prettiest, most decorated stall in the market.

In the morning, the villagers go to Maisie's workshop where Maisie is waiting for them.

'I'm feeling much better,' she says. 'I'll be able to serve my customers today, thanks to you all.'

The villagers carry all the Christmas decorations they have made over to Maisie's stall. Very soon, with the help of the villagers and the other stallholders, Maisie's stall is full of lovely decorations to sell. As soon as the market opens, Maisie has her first customer.

'You are all amazing,' says Maisie to the villagers, 'you've made my Christmas stall very special!'
'You helped us, Maisie, so we wanted to help you,' says Agnes Mouse.

The villagers take it in turn to help Maisie serve her customers, as well as enjoying the market.

By the end of the day, Maisie has sold almost every Christmas decoration.

She also wins a prize for the prettiest stall in market!

'This is the best Christmas ever,' says Agnes Mouse, when the villagers and Maisie are getting ready to go home.

'Yes, it is!' agrees Maisie. 'It's a magical Christmas and I've made lots of new friends.'

'Can we do it again next year, Maisie?' asks Mervyn Mouse.

'Yes, of course' replies Maisie, 'but without my arm in a sling!'

About this book

We are Mark (aka writer Jon Markes) and Nicky, owners of Cleggs, a small independent gift and homeware shop in York.

At Christmas time, our shop is known for its Christmas window display and decorations, sourced from around the world as well as many which are hand made by Nicky.

We published our first book, *Santa's Trousers,* in 2021, incorporating many of the Christmas felted animal decorations featured in a woodland scene for our window display. The book was such a success, we decided to write another for 2022 and *Maisie's Magical Christmas* is the result!

If you visit our shop you will see the Christmas market featured in the story, as well as Maisie and all the other characters. Some of the characters also appear in *Santa's Trousers.*

Characters featured in both books are available to purchase from:

Cleggs, 6 Goodramgate, York YO1 7LQ and cleggsyork.com

Cleggs illustration designed by Kirsty Crowder and used with permission

kirstycrowderillustrations.co.uk

Santa's Trousers

by Jon Markes

It's Christmas Eve and there is great excitement in the village. The villagers are waiting for Santa to come down from his house to switch on the Christmas tree lights.

But why is Santa sitting at home in his stripy underpants?

And who is wearing his trousers?

There is only one job left for Agnes Mouse to do.

She calls the grey mice to her cottage.

'Please take this basket of clean clothes to Santa,' she says, 'and make sure you hurry. We don't want Santa to be late switching on the Christmas tree lights.'

Santa takes his clothes out of the basket and puts them on. They smell fresh and clean.

'You look very handsome tonight, Santa, in your fresh clean clothes,' he says to himself.

But something is missing!

Printed in Great Britain
by Amazon

87389421R00016